Police and Thank You

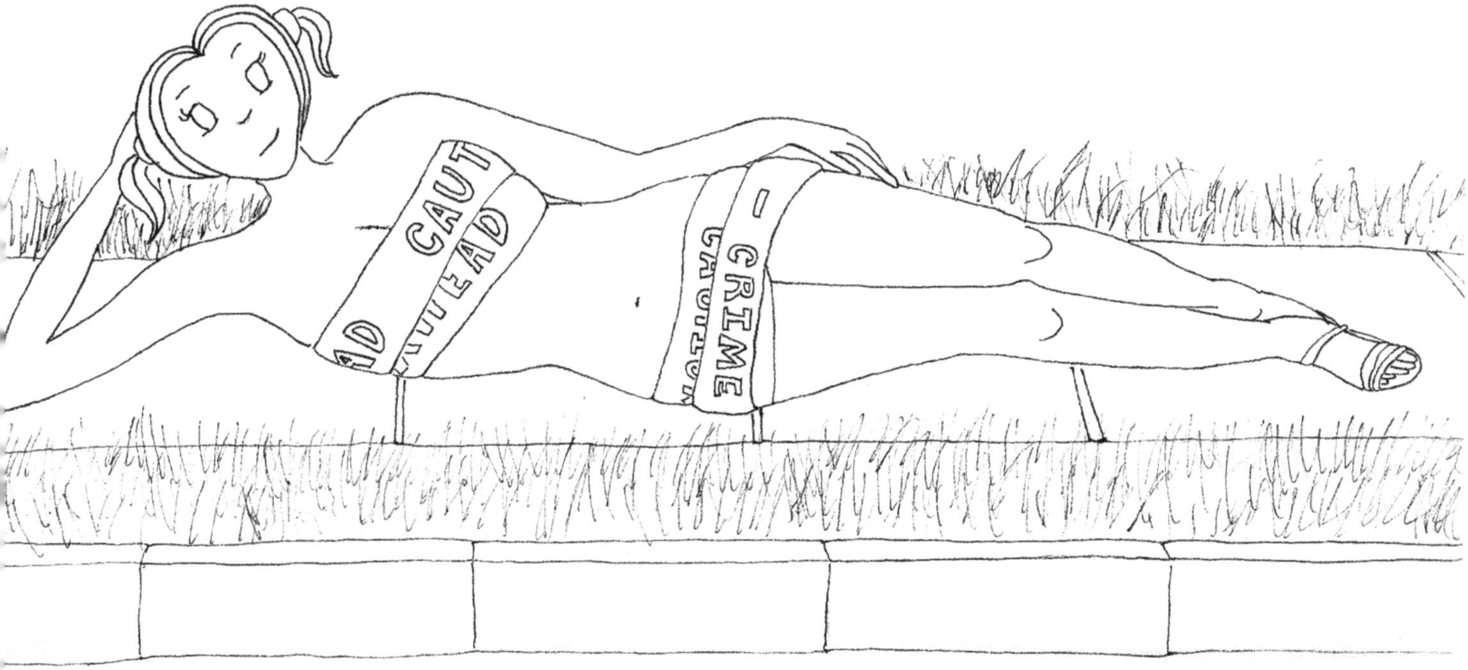

1

Hi there. Want a quick bite and a bump in the night?
No. But if you find me during business hours, I can help you treat your "night bumps" with pills.

Oh, come on. I have iron rich blood and great big veins. You could be in and out in no time.

Wait, I'm confused. Are you trying to sell me your body or your blood?

Which would you prefer?
Neither. Thank you.

What if I give you a discount?
No.
Do you and a friend at the same time?

I will not bite you in a snood. I will not bite you in the nude... Although I would look sensational in either.
Me too.

Officer, you won't believe what I just saw.
Was it a skinny guy with a low-cut top and questionable sexuality offering you body and soul in exchange for money?

How did you know that?
Tony works for us. He's undercover to help us catch vampires and get them off the streets.

I don't think that's right.
Why not? Vampires are murderers, aren't they?

That's not the point. If a vampire is minding his own business, and you trick him into committing a crime, how is that not entrapment?

It just... isn't. No one complains when we dress police women as prostitutes to lure lusty men to shame and arrest. And we've been doing that for years.

No. I'm pretty sure that's entrapment, too.
Shh.

Wouldn't it be more productive to go catch bad people rather than convince basically good people to break the law so you can arrest them?
Ideally, yes.

Practically, cops need to look busy, the department needs money, and good people pay their fines more often than bad people.
Don't you think that's a little unfair?

I get paid to think what the sheriff thinks. The sheriff thinks if you're right, you don't have to be fair.
Do you have kids, Officer Henderson?

My old lady and I haven't even talked about it, yet. Why?
Note to self: when next in Dr. Love's office, pick up more vasectomy coupons.

What in Gad's name are you wearing?
Caution tape. Some policemen are down the block doing a prostitution / vampire bust, and I'm going to try to have some fun with 'em.

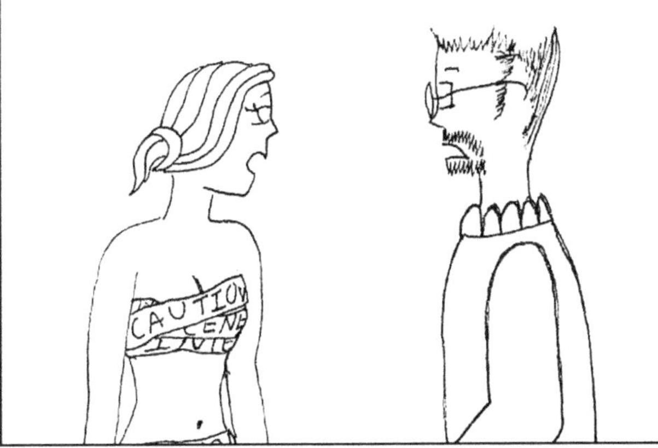

Just don't get arrested, please. Or they'll put our name in the paper, and we'll be in big trouble.
I don't expect to get arrested.

I'll probably hate myself for asking this, but isn't it uncomfortable wearing naught but plastic tape over your delicate bits?

Let's put it this way: I'm sweating, and I'm not going to tell you where.
What d'you know; mercy for the damned. Thank you, Lord.

Hey Henderson, isn't that the girl we saw earlier?
Sure is.

She's dead.
Freaky.

The perp's got a messed-up sense of humor; killing a woman, then dressing her up like a crime scene.

Should we call the coroner?
Of corse we should call the coroner, but...

Look, our shift's almost over, and she'll be just as dead in an hour or so. Let's leave her for someone else to find, huh?
Whatever, Man. Saves me some paperwork.

Blast! I should've waited 'til I was in custody to "play" dead. That county coroner looks good enough to eat.

Hey, Tony. What's up?
He bit me. Some guy actually bit me, and I need to know if it's a vampire bite.

Well, you're looking pale. You have pinpoint pupils, cold skin...
GASP!

I knew it. How much time do I have?
Here, quick! Look in the mirror, and see if your eye teeth have grown.

Is gullible really written on my forehead?
No. It's written on the mirror.

...but if you can see your reflection, it means what you got is probably not a vampire bite. What you've got there is a weirdo bite.

Do you think I'll turn into one of those?
Uh... let's take another look in the mirror, shall we?

If you've never been bitten before, where did all the puncture wounds come from?
When I was younger and hungrier, I did some screwy things for money.

Drugs?
No. Er... kind of. I volunteered for some medical studies and got stuck with a bunch of needles. I expect some of them were full of drugs.

Did anything disturbing happen to you?
Nah. The worst thing was worrying that someone might see my tattoo.

Okay. I have to ask. "Where," "Of what," and "Why?"
"Guess," "A metric ruler," and "Because 10 is greater than 4."

So this kid comes in after trying to get me arrested and wants treatment for a "vampire" bite.
Your handy work or someone else's?

Someone else's. But while I'm giving him his shots, he starts telling me how under the law, all vampires are serial murderers, so the justice system doesn't obligate itself to try them before they're sentenced.

Upsetting. Undead or not, you're still a citizen, right?
Wait. There's more.

The vampires get "life" sentences. Officially, they're all in prisons or exile. Unofficially, they get shipped God-knows-where to Navy SEALS, USMC, FBI... Anyone the government thinks isn't killing proficiently enough gets to practice on us.

That's appalling.
Isn't it, though?

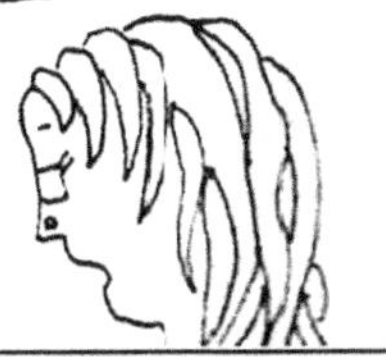

Are we going to stop 'em? You know, put on some flashy leather duds and pull off some kind of daring, implausible rescue?
No. I'm just giving the skeptics who don't think FAUST FORWARD would make a good feature film something to think about.

The Laughing Dead

Do you think other bosses send their chaplains to sexual harassment seminars?
I bet it happens more than you'd ever guess.

I once saw a list in a naughty panties catalog of places they'd discretely ship their merchandise. The country they listed right under "USA" was "Vatican City."

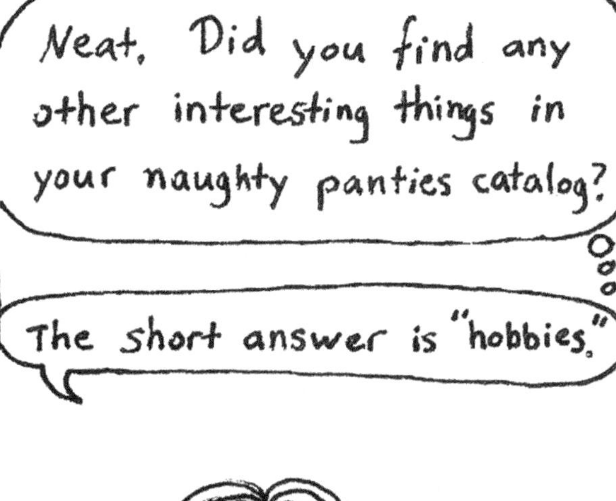

Neat. Did you find any other interesting things in your naughty panties catalog?
The short answer is "hobbies."

Would you like the long one?
If by "the long one" you mean "the strap-on one," no thanks.

When you feel things, does your body feel them, too?
He hasn't said. Why?

With all the vampires turning sissy in books and movies, the next step is zombie romance, and I have some sex questions.
Like what?

If zombies get frisky and bits of them fall off in the act, do their undead bodies lose feeling in the missing parts?
Um...

Or is there a reason Zombies are always moaning?
No Comment.

Hi there. Mary, right?
Do I know you?

We've never met, but I'm sinister, Dexter's better half.
Oh, the body! Hi.

"Better half" is a modest discription. You look more like Dexter's better nine tenths.
Very good.

Ironically, "nine tenths" under the law is "possession". Wanna see me turn my head around?
Never trust a funny zombie

Isn't it a little self-serving for vampires and supernatural beasties to work at a blood bank?
Maybe, but consider the alternative.

If we had to rummage around for food by our selves, we'd be killing people left and right.

As a blood bank, we give more than we take from the humans, all the donors are volunteers, and no one has to die unless we want them to.
DO you want them to?

Some of them. That's how we ended up with an organic food court.
Ooh, liver and onions!

You don't trust me, do you?
I really don't.
Why is that?

Dexter is smart, grounded, and amazing. And I think there's a reason you and he aren't together anymore.

Would you believe "we just grew apart"?
No.

How about "I think of Dexter as the one that got away"?
I think I'm starting to loose my respect for the dead.

Let me come to the point. I want you to bite me.
Why's that, Mr. Sinister?

You and I both defy mortal boundries like death, but you don't do it in a perpetual state of decay.

I'm tired of watching myself decompose a little each day, and if you bite me, perhaps your vampire venom will keep me from falling apart.
That sounds risky. What if I refuse to bite you?

Then I'll bite you and let you catch what I have.
The joke's on him. Stupid's not contagious.

Why do you want to bite me, Mr. Sinister? There are other vampires around.
Sorry, Lady. I'm a predator. I have to pick prey that I can catch.

I see. I'm a girl and alone and...
Strong preys on weak. Weak preys on weaker. You know how it is.

Do you know who Mefisto is?
I've never met the guy.
He's not a guy.

He's the devil figure in the German epic, FAUST. Mefisto persuades Faust. to sell his soul in exchange for happiness.
I didn't know that. And I'd be lying if I said I cared.

Well, you should care, because Mefisto is also...

SMACK!

...the delivery vehicle for a knuckle sandwich.
Ah, like "My-fist-o." I find your humor rye.

Fearing a lawsuit after the mishap with Mr. Sinister, Mary's boss sends her to a psychiatrist.
Do you know what triggered this irrational fear of Zombies?
When they find me at work and want to make me one of them, it's a rational fear of zombies.

When you say "Zombies," do you mean you see the human race as mindless and as trying to conform you? To make you Zombie-like?
Doctor, I really am a vampire, and I really did get assaulted by a REAL zombie. And we'll get results faster in these sessions if you read my file.

Okay. E-hem.
"Subject displays tendencies toward rapid-swing bipolar disorder as evidenced by severe reactions to normal stressors.
Self-reports history of depression, hypersexuality, suicide, and homicide as well as..."

Holy Cow!
Either Dr. Michaels is summoning the god of beef vindaloo, or he found my dental x-rays.

Are psychiatrists really all sex-obsessed and lonely?
Who's analyzing whom, Miss Faust?
I meant no disrespect, Doctor.

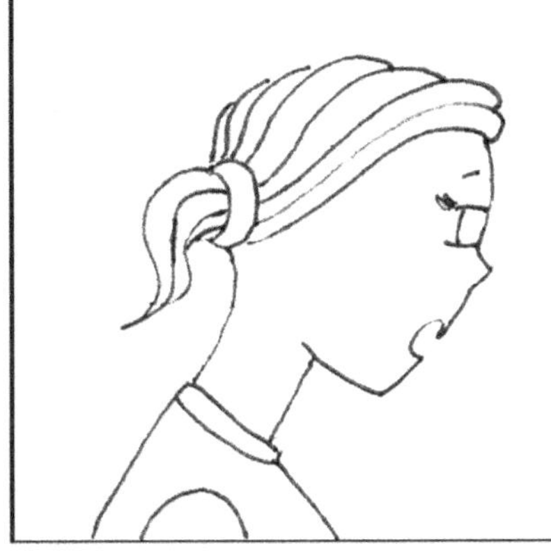

In the psych books I've read, Freud thought all human action was toward the avoidance of pain or the seeking of sexual pleasure. What do you think?

I think psychology has come a long way since Sigmund Freud. My goal is to find out why people think what they think, then give them theraputic amounts of knowledge and medication so they can...

Must you sit on my couch like that?
Who's a-Freud of the big, bad womb?

I know what you're doing, Miss Faust. You're testing the boundaries of my intellect and personal comfort by playing with me.
Can you blame me, Doctor?

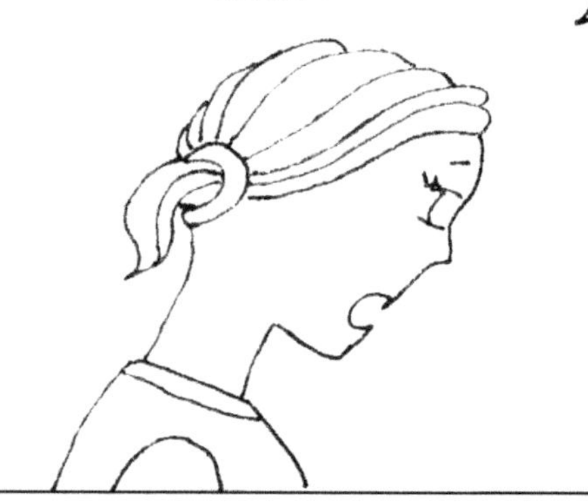

I bet a lot of your patients think they're clever and complicated, but I really am. So if I wanted help, I'd be most likely to get it from someone who's a little sharper than I am.

For example, if you wanted to probe for the source of my negative body image, I'd probe right back for why a mild-mannered psychiatrist drives to work in a red Corvette with blue leather interior.
No need to probe. I drive a custom car for the same reason I play a mean piano:

Great performance is not based on the size of the keys.
If I laugh at this pianist, it won't be the first.

And that's how your body's neck got broken. Sorry for hurting him, but I didn't know what else to do.
It's truly okay, Mary.

If you hadn't, we wouldn't have known just how much of his work he'd been taking home with him.
Brain worm eat thought.
Um, what?

You know how Dr. S's caution and common sense on a project are inversely proportionate to how much of other people's money he can spend on it?
Yeah.

Well, his new thing is genetically enhanced parasites; "Brain worms," so he can start the zombie epidemic, then cure it later for a price.

This little guy got free and wandered into Sinister's right ear. He's been telling him what to do for weeks.
Crazy.

You're thinking of all the people you'd like to buy a brain worm tequila, aren't you?
Aren't you?

So you're the little worm that's going to father the zombie generation?
Yes'm. I'm gonna be the badest thing to hit humanity since typhoid, polio, or veggie cheese, And from such humble beginnings.

Why? What were you before?
Greedy geneticists and the pervy old men who fund them thought my growth potential could be used to fight erectile dysfunction.
The plan was to turn me into a local injection like Botox, kind of. Then...

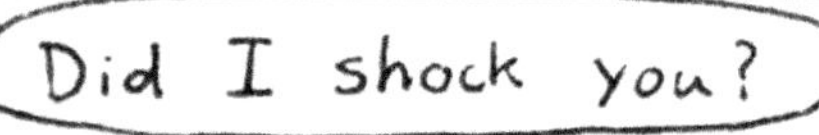

Did I shock you?
No. I just thought of what to call you on the TV commercials, but I don't want to say it. I'm sorry I even thought it.
Well, it's not like you're going to offend me, so spit it out.

WORMWOOD.
Feel better?
No.

Looking for something?
No. Making something.
Type. type. type.
Type. type. type. type. type.
I met the parasite that's going to cause the zombie uprising, and I'm trying to over come some fears by making fun and profit out of the whole thing.
Type. type. type. type. type.
Type. type. type.
"Worried about undead legions taking over?
Do scary stiffs have you scared stiff?
Quit your worrying (because it won't do any good) and kiss your butt goodbye in style with NEW APOCALYPSTICK, available in red, black, white, and pale."
That does it!
Step aside, Sister. No one writes anything THAT absurd on MY computer but ME.
Nothing breaks your writer's block up into manageable pieces like seeing someone write something you wish you thought of.

Shelley and Dexter are zombies in a way. Why aren't you scared of them?
Shelley's not contagious, and Dexter wasn't synthesized in a lab.

The voodoo inspired zombies from back in the good old days had resurrection for a purpose. They were sacred. But when you start manufacturing minions de la muerte like motor cars or spandex shorts, it seems really wrong to me.

"Lab synthesized" or "lab altered" doesn't mean "evil" necessarily. Do you think mold is better than penicillin because mold is natural

No.
Do you think surgeon sculpted bosoms are better than God-made bosoms because they came from a lab?
Okay. You've got me there.

You wanted to see me, Doctor?
Yes, I did. Have I told you lately that you're irresistible?
Dr. Gregory
RS
10: -- whenever

Um, no. I've thrown myself at you semi annually for 10 years, and you've found me pretty resistible so far.
Ah, Mary, come to my place after work. I want to be in your head, in your heart, under your skin...

Wow. This is sudden. I guess I always hoped you'd look up and see me one day, and... Wait, "in my head"? "Under my skin"? Turn your head for a minute, would you, Doc?

Uh-huh. That's what I thought. You can come out now, Wormwood. The fun's over.
Aw, man!

I thought zombie contagions only attacked dead tissue. Why are you nomming the neurons out of the man of my dream's temporal lobe?
Do I look like a picky eater? Food is food.
Well you can find plenty of food in the morgue. Now beat it.

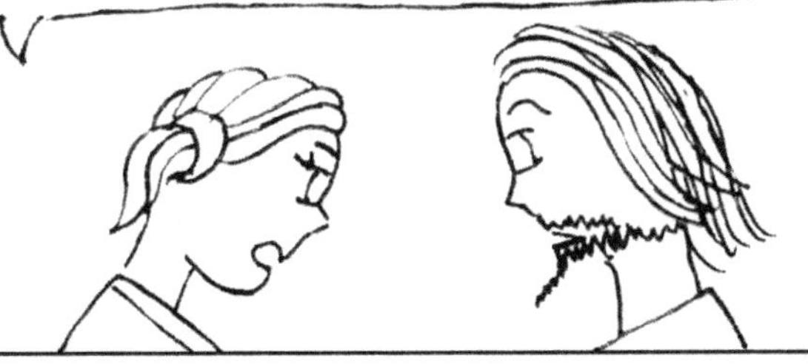

What was I saying?
You were going to re-route the money from the Compound Z Project to one that's less socially irresponsible, like Better Honey through Killer Bees, or The All Piranha Petting Zoo.

Cheer up, kiddo. Dr. Gregory may have slipped through your fingers, but you still have me.
It's not fair.

But its honest. The trouble with you is you have too many scruples to enjoy the man you adore unless HE adores YOU of his own free will.

Stupid scruples!
Stupid indeed, but it's your own silly fault for not letting me work my brain matter magic in peace.

"Live and let lobe," I always say.
Shut up.

Doctor, do you remember my asking you a while back if you were married, betrothed, or gay?
Mm - hmm.

How about crazy or stupid?
What's on your mind, Mary?

...ack then, you blew me off and said you n't date co-workers. Fine. My hopes nd day dreams haven't been the same ince, but I was fine with respecting your wishes...

...until your pal the brain worm loosened your tongue, and you rattled off a bunch of romantic weirdness and mixed me way the heck up on how to feel and act around you.

SO, since our working relationship's going to be awkward now, anyway, I'd like to help you figure out what your REAL hang-up is about me, because I'm fantastic, and employer or not, any man who doesn't want me is crazy, stupid, married, betrothed, or gay.

Is it too late to say "I don't remember"? That "Wormwood ate the memory of what I said to you"?
See, that's why I haven't ruled out "stupid."

What happened? I thought you were going to bring in something hansome.
That was the plan, but Hansome doesn't date employees.

You don't have any size 31 love potions, do you?
I do, but they rarely end well for anyone, and my potions only work for me.

Is that what caused all your man trouble?
Hey, if Mother wanted me to be well-behaved, she'd have named me "Virginia," not "Jezebel."

Nah. I think that would have made things worse.
So, maybe I'd lose the "Vir" and keep the "gin."

I want to give you a bizarre but sincere compliment.
Okay. Shoot.

200 years ago, you would have been burned at the stake for being so clever.
Thank you.

But 200 years ago, we both would've had stakes with our names on them.
HOLY

The difference is your stake would be rare, and mine would be well-done.
It takes a witch to make a pun seem magical.

Then, she got really upset with me, and now, I'm stuck. I can't fire her, but I need to be able to treat her like an employee.
Well, you did tell her to come home with you, and you did know how she felt about you.

But that was under the affects of Compound Z. I didn't mean to hurt her feelings.

Good intentions may win you brownie points in Heaven, but most of your associates here on Earth aren't impressed by what you mean to do. All that matters to them is what you do.

What do you think my odds are of living this down any time soon?
The same as the odds of my learning to whistle, whisper, or hop on one leg.

Now that Wormwood left, do you think you and Sinister will get back together again?
I'm a "never say never" kind of guy, but there are a lot of hurt feelings to overcome, and that takes time.

Forgiveness would come easier if I believed he was sorry, but I don't think he IS sorry. I think he just misses the things I could do for him.

Do you still consider yourself a sexual being even though you have no body or mate?
You bet I do.

My palm gets sweaty whenever I think of Chinese finger traps.
I feel the same way about elevator buttons.

Work Sucks

What's with the not-roses?
A gift from Dr. Michaels. He asked if he could put me in his next book and gave me a cactus.

She's called "the queen of the night," and she's nocturnal like me. Her breed of cactus blooms at night so it can be pollinated by bats.

Well, I think it's bad taste to take gifts from your psychiatrist, even the creepy ones.
I'm glad you said something, my spicy little Pepper...

...because I think it's important to listen to the criticism of my peers, even the crabby ones.
PTHHH!

If God had made men from wood instead of clay, how would he have attached the feet?
I don't know. How?

With toe nails.
Yick! Your jokes are as bad as my brother's.

Have a heart, Mary. People at work expect me to be a piety figure. I'm trying to keep my jokes clean.
Sorry. I bet that's quite a challenge.

You could even call it a handicap, if you like.
I so don't

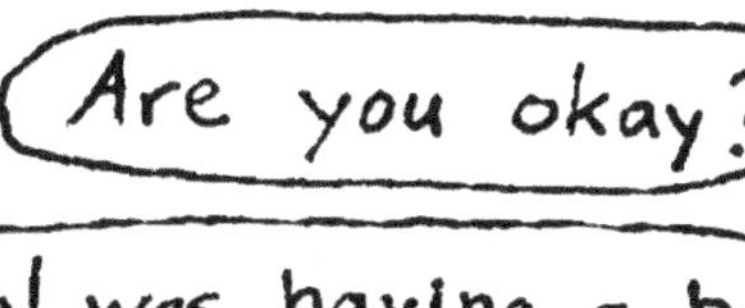

Are you okay?
Cybal was having a bad day, so I told her your dorky "toenails" joke

Did that make it worse?
No. I got her to smile, but Pepper was there and in one of her moods.

What happened?
She got uppitty and rude because I "used the Lord's name in vain" and told me to leave her floor; that she'd had enough of my "negativity."

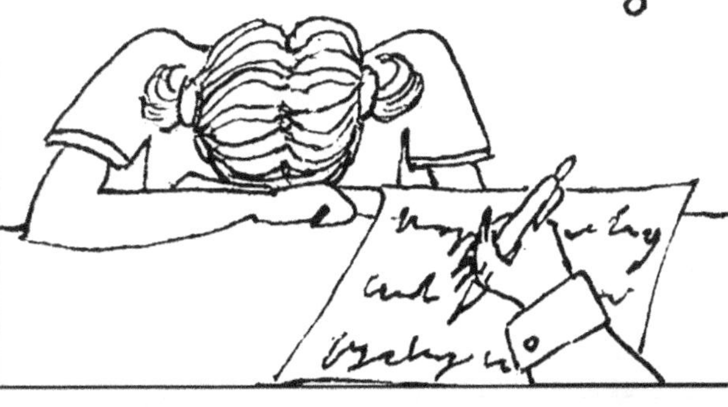

Do you ever have nights like this?
Ya-huh. You'd be amazed at how many co-workers I'd like to acquaint with the sound of "one hand slapping."

You look troubled.
I just saw Pepper a minute ago.

Uh - oh. What's she done now?
She, uh, hugged me.

You're kidding.
Nope. She said she was sorry for the misunderstanding the other day and that she, get this, appreciates me.
Weird.

Almost makes you wish you hadn't nominated her for the KEVORKIAN AWARD, in the malpractice category doesn't it?
Almost.

So, I was giving Mr. Fields an intravenous treatment, and I hung it on one of our rolling poles like, you know, we do...
Ya?

And I got to thinking that these porn makers and dance clubs have it all wrong with their naughty nurse acts. With a little practice and some adjustments for having a prop that moves, they could come up with some pretty unusual routines.

If you're going to ask for my blessing to become the first vampiric, pole-dancing, top-dropping night nurse, you can forget it.

But I'd make tons of money, and I'd never get hurt.
It's a bad idea.
I could call myself "Poison I V."
Don't.

After years of frustration at work, Mary starts exploring employment options.
I'm sorry, Miss Faust. The KEVORKIAN INSPIRED LAUD LEAGUE cannot offer you a job on our panel of judges.

But I'm qualified. I'm MORE than qualified.
In euthanasia. I know. I read your resume.

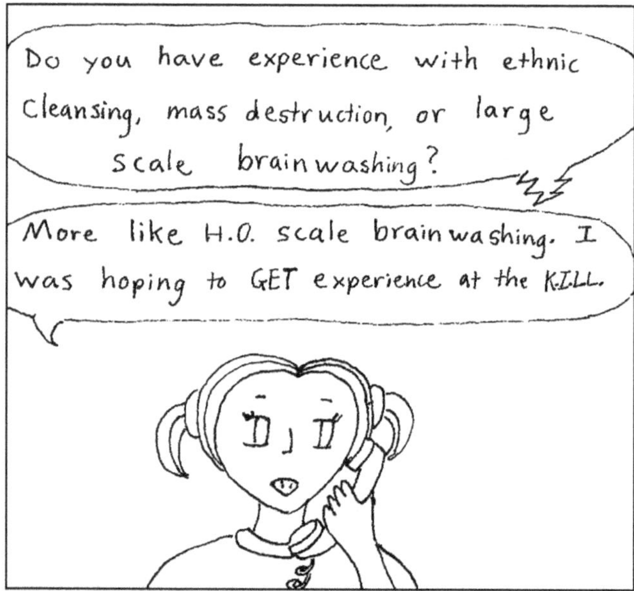

Do you have experience with ethnic cleansing, mass destruction, or large scale brainwashing?
More like H.O. scale brainwashing. I was hoping to GET experience at the KILL.

We used to do that kind of thing. But Kevorkian awarders are trending toward global menaces because genocidal maniacs like to be judged by OTHER genocidal maniacs.

And anyway, you're a girl.
That wasn't very nice.

I'm a genocidal maniac. I'm not supposed to be nice.

As work continues to suck more and more, Mary dreams of moving to Transylvania.
Grad, this place is boring!
Surprised?

I was hoping there would be more gothic murkiness in Romanian culture, but it's all quiet quaintness.

Not full of impalers like Vlad, is it?
Not at all.

The reason we hear about Good Ol' Vlado is that he WASN'T normal. I don't think normal Romanians quite appreciate how their historical figures have turned into horror icons.

Pity.
Is it? Do you think they'd do that to our history?

Meanwhile in Springfield...
LINCOLN
Look Mama, it's ze wampire slayer from ze movie.
Why couldn't a neat guy like that come from Transylwania?

Here's something interesting. "Romania's 'Merry Cemetery' is famous for its colourful gravestones which are decorated with paintings and funny epitaphs for the dead."
That's cool.

And the city of Brasov (pronounced [brŏ·zŏff], I assume) is home to the grandest gothic church east of Vienna.
That's... not quite as cool.

Hang on. "This church is called 'The Black Church,' and has the largest organ in Europe."

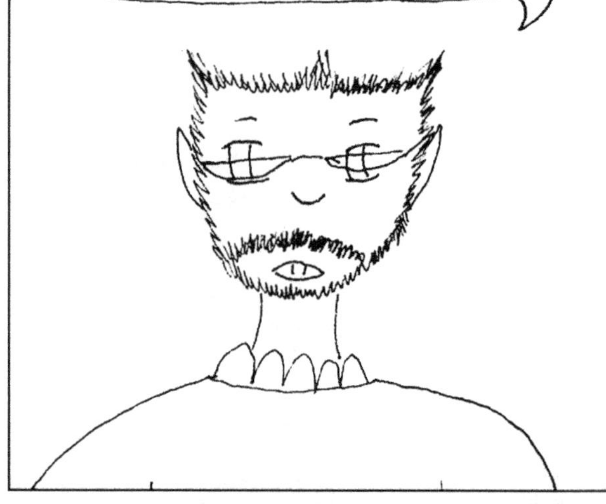

Ya-huh. I'll bet Europe's largest organ would get lots of [brŏ·zŏff].

How DARE you?!
I get that a lot. Can you be more specific?

"Dear Ms. Malone, The Kevorkian..." blah, blah, blah, "...invites you to accept our coveted 'Jackie' award for euthanasia expertly disguised as malpractice."
Is this or is this NOT your doing?

That might have been me.
I have never euthanized anyone! How dare you make a mockery of my professional misfortunes?

Either accept the award like you did it on purpose or admit to the world you're incompetent.

Later, at The Jackies...
I'd like to thank my mother's work ethic, my father's indifference, and my little club foot without which this honor would not have been possible.

Pepper Dear, a chicken-fried steak at a fat farm is in less danger than a patient in your care. 11 people have died in the last 3 years because you erred on the side of laziness while treating them.

Peter and the Wolfgirl

An Ode to Writer's Block
by
Peter Faust

My writer's block is sturdier than tungsten, iron, or steel. No river can erode it, and no lava can congeal to form a craggy mountain or a formidible rock enough to rival my unyielding awesome writer's block.

My writer's block is doubtlessly my hero's dearest friend. It keeps the villain helpless, so there's no need to extend his sword in mortal combat for a damsel under lock and key, or even scuff his armor, thanks to writer's block.
My writer's block is massive. Yet, it's lighter still than air. More constant than a freckle, more unruly than a bear, it's exhausted all my calendars and run down every clock, but it is mine, and I am its: my fit of writer's block.

But you don't HAVE writer's block! You're writing NOW!
Am not.
I've just painted letters on a bunch of little writer's blocks and started forming words with 'em.

Men are uncouth hounds in heat every day and night of the year,

44

What's this?
I'll give you a hint. It starts with a "B."

No. There's something stuck to it.
* Peel *
It's a quarter. Your butt is growing quarters.

I don't think so. I must've sat on it.
Is there any more?
Hey, beat it, Buster. Those are my hind quarters.

You see? It wasn't all bad.
Are you married? And if not, Would you like to be?

Once in a while, my sister says men are pigs, and when she does, it's usually because someone she cared about was mean to her.
Sniff.

Don't cry, Rosie. Whoever he is, I promise he's not worth it.
He used to be. That's what makes it hurt so bad.

Just for my information, should a man be more concerned if the heartbroken woman thinks he's a pig or if she thinks he's a dog?

It depends. Is she craving Mandarin or Korean?
I wonder if it's too late to wok away from this conversation.

Forgive my prying, but your one-time love wasn't named Adam Edwards, was he?
How did you know that?

I got a hunch from the way you described him. He burned my sister Mary pretty bad a few years back. She cried for weeks.

I'm sorry.
It's not your fault. It's his. That's one Adam I'm truly surprised hasn't been split, yet.

Maybe if Mary and I each grabbed a leg and pulled real hard...
My sub atomic particles hurt just thinking about it.

I'll tell you what. I'll agree men are dogs if you'll concede some dogs are loyal and affectionate, not uncouth humping machines.
Grr...

If you don't, it's like if I say "women are snarling, moody hormone factories," when I know lots of them aren't, including you.

The only reason you're like that right now is the full moon and the cheap beer. Tomorrow morning, you'll look and feel like a sweetie again.
True. On my less contrary days, I like to think of myself as mostly woman, not mostly werewolf.

Less K-9, more femi-9?
I don't like you, Dude. But I'll probably use that line when I'm sober and have time to forget you said it.

So I guess Adam has spent the last 3 years breaking more hearts and teaching other girls to hate men.
I wish I was like Cerce, the Sorceress. Then, I could turn disrespectfull men into pigs.

That implies they weren't ones already. Could it be my little sister is mellowing out on her "men are pigs" stance?

Not especially. I'm just sorry that from Ancient Greece to here and now, women have been as antagonized by men as I am.
And I'm sure for almost that long, Men like me have been defending men like me attitudes like yours.

On the other hand, pigs are bacon. And if men are pigs, I'd still rather be bacon than eggs. "Girls" are still "Chicks," right?
My big brother has been known to make as many as 6 insufferable wisecracks before breakfast.

You said your friend from the bar is Rosie Carter?
That's what she told me. Why?

She's a beauty queen.
"Miss Baskerville," right?

No. "Miss Sweet Sensations." Roseanne Carter has been the spokes model for McCavity's Candy Company. for 2 years running. Look.
Son of a gun.

You thought she was just a dog, didn't you?
Kinda.

How can your hair turn into such a tangled mess in a single night?
Mr. McCavity thinks I should be able to groom myself when I get through "changing."

If he treated his pets like this, he'd be arrested.
His pets are thoroughbreds. I'm a rescue. He doesn't owe me anything.

Is modeling all he expects in exchange for room and board?
On Sundays, we dress up and play "The Sugar Plum Fairy and the Black-hearted Licorice Whipper."

Please don't tell me which is which.
I'm kidding.

You don't seem too happy about living here. Why don't you leave?
I don't know where I'd go.

2 years ago, I was literally a stray. I didn't want my lycanthropy to hurt good people, so I chased them away.

Mr. McCavity offered me a job knowing I'd work cheap because when he found me, I was a hitchhiker trying to catch a ride outside his store.
I've hitchhiked before. That's not an easy thing to do.

It's worse when you're a thumb-sucker like me.
That's easily the most adorable lie I've ever heard.

So the thing with Adam was...
An escape, I think; not liking my life and trying on a different one.

I'm over it now.
Are you? 'Cause I think you're a time bomb.

Is that a fact?
Mm-hmm. The difference between dogs and wolves is wolves don't beg.

You are begging for your meals from a man you hate and suppressing the instinct to hunt for something better.

Pretty soon, you'll want to escape again and odds are good you'll try it with another worthless man. I'll be waiting at the end to brush your hair and bring you coffee some more if you wish.

In the mean time, I'll put away any fantasies I had about you and me sharing champagne and a flea bath.
Tick bath, my sweet. Time bombs have ticks.

Peter came in this morning asking for some hangover juice. Is he okay?
He's fine apart from the handful of spooky women and unfinished books in his head.

He talks about writer's block a lot, but he's NOT blocked exactly. He's just stuck on his kooky poems and won't go back to the novels.
He might be afraid to.
HOLY Grounds

In order for Peter to write the kind of fiction he wants to write, he has to go to some dark places in his mind and stay there until the story's done.
Maybe he should be a cartoonist. Then, he could be as dark as he wants and never have to go more than 4 frames without a punchline.

Who reads cartoons?
More people than poetry, I hope.
HOLY Grounds

MCCAVITY CANDY CO. closed its doors today following accusations that Chairman Kenneth McCavity is involved in slave trafficking hit the news. McCavity told police his workers are not slaves but tiny were-creatures purchased legally in their dog form and brought here from Nepal.

The public defender's office issued a statement saying McCavity's ploy toward pleading insanity will not work.

Our reporters wanted Miss Sweet Sensations herself, Roseanne Carter's side of the story but were unable to locate her. They do know she left the McCavity Mansion and entered The Motel Maine with two of her tiny co-workers last night. They were not found there, but a startled housekeeper swears she saw a werewolf in a quivering dog pile with two Jack Russell Terriers in their room.

Melody awoke.

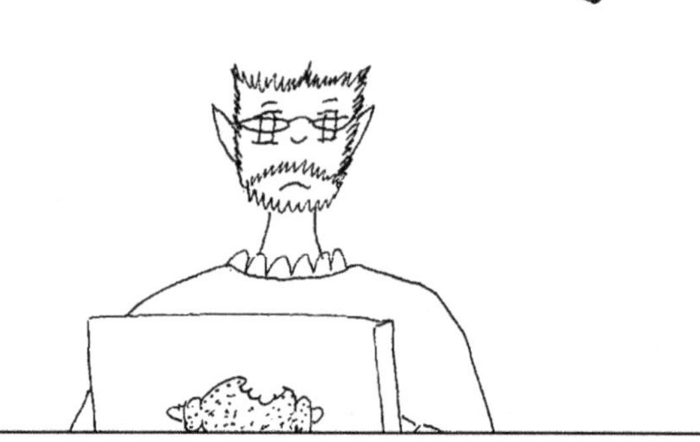

She had hoped that when she did, IF she did, it would be in the Heaven she had heard about when she was a little girl.

Instead, she felt the constriction of leather straps under her chin, ribs, and hips binding her to a cold, metal table.
She knew now that she'd been a fool to trust Dr. Levine, for instead of easing her over the threshold from this life into the next like he'd promised, he had brought her in her sleep to this shabbily lit dungeon with its peeling paint, green tiles, and no windows.
Somewhere around a corner or in the shadows just out of sight was Dr. Levine, the cunning, cruel mastermind who had no doubt convinced the world she was dead. There would be no one to look for her and no one to help her.

Is that the story you're dedicating to Rosie?
Yep.

Woman hath no fury like a writer scorned, I guess.

So she got away from you, huh?
Go away.

It's just as well. You know what your problem is?
A proclivity for meeting kooks at the bar?

You thought you could give Rosie freedom by getting her out of that mad house she's in, but that's not how she sees things.
How does she see things, Adam?

Like McCavity's a man with a cage, and you're a man with a leash.
I see.

So you think it's better to leave her in the cage until you're ready to play with her?
How else would you get a woman to respond?

TACKLE!
SUBDUE!
INCARCERATE!
Lh...mrr... rrdr...hr!
There. See how much fun this isn't?

Hello. May I speak to Peter, please?
Speaking.

Peter! It's me, Rosie.
Mm-hmm. I read about your 3 dog night in the paper. Did your animal instincts land you in the pound?

No. In the dumpster.
I don't believe you.

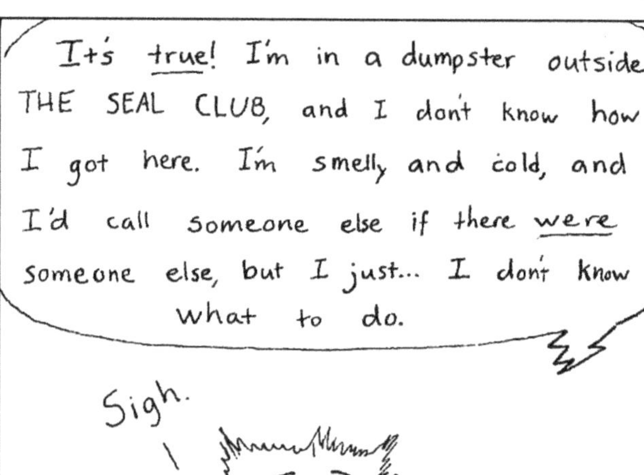

It's true! I'm in a dumpster outside THE SEAL CLUB, and I don't know how I got here. I'm smelly and cold, and I'd call someone else if there were someone else, but I just... I don't know what to do.
Sigh.

Why don't you come to my place? You can take a shower and use Mary's room while she's at work.
Um...
Don't worry. I'll keep busy or make myself scarce. I will be a perfect gentleman.

Then, what's the point?
Good question.

After learning Rosie will be sleeping over, Mary reacts the way every loving, supportive sister reacts to her brother's chivalrous behavior.
You stupid git!

Not the kind of reassurance I was hoping for.
The girl of your dreams is vulnerable, horny, and spending the night. Why are you still typing?

What should I be doing?
How about drop to one knee and say "Thank you, Powers-that-be, for choosing me out of all the critters in all the world and gifting me with a happy ending"?

It's not a happy ending. It's a trick. I don't believe in happy endings.
That's not a good enough reason to pass up an opportunity like this.

Maybe one'll come to me while I'm writing.
Well, if you change your mind, there are some you-know-whats on the counter. They have poetry printed on them.

Thanks, but I can't see myself getting hot and bothered in a condom with "Leaves of Grass" on it.
How about "The Man from Nantucket"?

Slay it ain't So

Thou mockest now but not for long, for I am "Bloodgroove, Slayer of vampires."

Are you sure you're not "Steve, Bagger of Groceries"? You look like "Steve, Bagger of Groceries."

Look, Steve...
Bloodgroove, Slayer of Vampires!
Let me bring you up to speed on some things.
You are tresspassing in the domain of a critter who eats men's hearts for breakfast and studies torture techniques in its spare time.
Can you give me one good reason why I shouldn't unzip your skin and juice you like an orange?

Wait, you CAN'T drink my blood. I have, uh...
... Sickle cell anemia!

Drat.
That's not going to work, is it?
No, it isn't. Would you like to try "Ovarian cancer"?

Ring.
Ring
Hello?

Ugh.
I mean...
Adam!
Hi.

Ya. I figured you were Back in town when your brother showed up and tried to kill me.
Mind? Not at all. I know you'd never send, say, Flowers like a non-crazy person.

You'd like to go out when?
I'm sorry. I can't.

I'm having coffee with my landlord.
I never mind meeting your friends. It's just the ones that bug me never taste as much like pepperoni as I think they should.

So that's how the window got smashed in. Sorry for having to call you about this.
Don't worry about it. The house is insured. And if a broken window is the worst thing that happens to you in a slayer encounter, it's a good day.

I guess so. Do you ever feel bad about having to dispatch the well-meaning nit-wits who want to destroy you?
Once in a LONG while.

Believe it or not, I tend to get sentimental around the holidays occasionally about the women who have crossed my path.

What do you do about it?
I look up their pictures and remind myself how malice-filled and insane they were. Then, I send them off in Christmas cards. I think of them as my "slay belles."

Do dragons fear the afterlife?
"Afterlife" means something different to dragons.

Humans look at death as the end. They have to sweat time constraints more than someone who thinks "death" is just birth into another form of life.

Humans also worry about being judged by their maker. Dragons, with our indestructable egos and immaculate self-image, have a hard time seeing ourselves being weighed in the balance and found wanting.

Would the Almighty have to weigh dragons in the balance, or could he just look at the scales?
Humph!
I'm not actually sulking. I'm just giving my cheeky friend the privilege of seeing my profile.

Do you ever envy those legendary dragons who seized money and power rather than doing business with mortals for it?
Dragons don't like money as such.

We like GOLD because dragons are kind of vain, and we think we deserve the best, but money isn't that appealing to us. You can't eat it, you can't build a house with it...

There must be something charming about it. Otherwise, why bother being such a reliable landlord?
I make as much money as I can so the humans don't get it and use it to do irresponsible things.
What would you use it for?

I'd buy the naming rights to all the stars and re-name each one Ignatius after my own, dear self.
Saying "dragons are kind of vain" is like saying "appendicitis is kind of uncomfortable."

You're up early.
I can't sleep.

I've tried everything from counting sheep to pure poison. None of the usual stuff is helping.
Would you like to try some ambient noise, like whale songs or wind chimes? Winthrop just loaned us his Sounds of the Rainforest album.

How about an album of screams? I bet I could doze off if I could listen to some bone-chilling, blood-curdling, sphincter-clenching screams for an hour or so.

Is Adam back in town?
How EVER did you guess?

How's Steve?
Better after the transfusion.

That was very unkind sending your brother to my house dressed as a slayer.
What's the harm? You got a free lunch, Steve got some much-needed experience with women...

...and I got to have a kinky, interuption-free date with a not-you girl with-out having to worry about you showing up and making a scene.

In fact, I think you owe me a heart-felt "thank you."
That wasn't my plan.

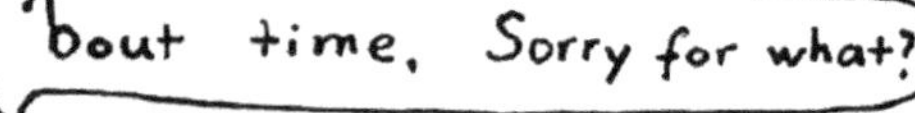

However, I did pick THIS up for you in the gift shop. It's an "I'm sorry" present.
'bout time. Sorry for what?
WHAP!

That.
I think you broke my nose.
Then have two presents; one for each nostril.

I know you don't take my suggestions seriously, Miss Faust, but if you practice some self-control at work, you'll get sent to see me a lot less.
I take your suggestions seriously, Doctor. I've been more conscious of my mood osculations since you talked to me about them.

I talked to you about your mood oscillations. "Osculation" is, like "kissing."
Is it? I thought that's when you get real skinny.

That's "emaciation."
No, no. That's when you cut off body parts.

I'm pretty sure that's "emasculation."
See? I also took you seriously when you said you wanted to try some word association.
Why couldn't my mother have wanted me to be an anesthesiologist?

Do psychiatrists still hypnotize people with pendulums?
Not usually.

Results from things like that are questionable because it's hard to prove if what the patient tells us is repressed memory or if it's something conjured up from subconscious suggestion. Why?

A friend says she got pendulum boobs after having kids, and I thought "Gee, that would be a cunning way to get men interested in mental health; just start hypnotizing them with breasts.

Of course that notion works best if the psychiatrist is a woman.
I'll pass that idea along to my female colleagues the next time I need to be slapped.

Has anyone ever talked to you about subduing those "say whatever you want" impulses?
Folks don't tend to stick around long enough to tell me about myself.

Could you be chasing people away with shear tactlessness?
I could, but I don't intend to stop.

I like honesty, and I get it so seldom that I feel like I need to be extra blunt to compensate for the rest of the world.

Lonely road, that. Most people won't know how to handle someone who speaks Id-dish as fluently as you.
It's an ugly but efficient language. Like German.

After learning his sister Mary had been threatened by a slayer, Peter Faust insists on teaching Mary self-defense
You've got to be kidding

Why do I have to fight in high-heeled shoes? I feel ridiculous.
You're not ridiculous. You're deadly

Think about it. Would you rather be stepped on by an elephant or an elephant wearing stilettoes?
I've honestly never thought about it.

Trust me, Sister Dear. Based on force and weight distribution, you can do way more damage when you fight in these shoes instead of your flats.

Then why aren't YOU wearing high heels?
Now, now.

Ha-HAH, thou vixen of viciousness, I have returned to claim you for death and hell.
Neat. While you do that, can I claim you for nut and case?

Your jests shall not save you, for I, Bloodgroove, have prevailed against your nigh fatal wound and have sworn on my honor to end you.
Now get this.

Up to now, I've been nice. I've let you live hoping you'd learn something from these absurd suicide missions on which you try to kill me. This time, when you fail, I believe I'll gift you with "life" as I know it. What do you think of that?
But then I'll be a vampire. I hate vampires. I'm predestined to kill them.

I'll be just like BLADE.
You mean a stupid slayer in a stupid comic with a highly flawed plot based on older, BETTER vampire stories?
Nah!

You're not finishing my book for me by any chance, are you?
I wouldn't dare.

I started thinking ahead to the day I meet a skillful slayer and thought I'd better have a will and burial arrangements ready.
That's a sad thought. Accurate, but sad.

I'm looking for a gravesite next to someone with a headstone shaped like a heart because I want my headstone to be shaped like a bladder.

That sounds like a tasteless, expensive sight gag.
And I want it engraved with the words "When you gotta go, you gotta go."

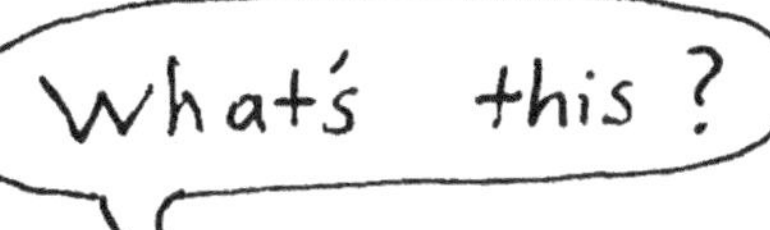

What's this?
The flowers came for you while you were out.

Bleeding hearts and a tent stake, huh?
Yup. I think they're from your slayer friend.

I don't have a slayer friend. I have a bumbling, idiotic, kind-of-sort-of stalker who thinks he's Van Helsing's smarter offspring, but couldn't hurt a fly if he had the guts to try it.

Well, whatever he is, he sent you flowers. Take a look at the card.
"I'm crazy about you in a non-homicidal way." That's all I need.

Panel 1

Panel 2

Panel 3

Panel 4

Hi, Grandma. I brought you flowers.
I won't lie. I didn't buy them, but I got them from a man I don't like very much, and I couldn't think of anyone who deserves them more.
I've done some remarkable things since my fall from grace. You wouldn't be proud of all of them, but some of them, I hope you would be.
With all the supernatural stuff I can see now, I sort of hoped I'd run into you, someday.
I love you. I miss you.
Maybe the fact that I haven't means you really DID go to a better place, huh?
Burst!
Marguite
Eek!!!
Dexter,
I wonder how you say "Boo" in sign language.
I love you somewhat less than I did a minute ago.

You shouldn't have to worry about your Grandma being proud of you, you know.
No. I don't know.

By virtue of my vampirehood, God is and will always be mad at me, if you take the folklore keepers seriously.

My Grandma was a good lady who, I hope, ended up on the Heaven side of eternity, and I worry SHE might feel the way God does.

Well, the actual choice to turn vampiric didn't hurt anyone but you. And I've watched some pretty evil people turn and repent. I don't believe you're any less forgivable than they are.

So what brings you to the cemetery besides scaring the wits out of your friends?
When I feel down, I stand next to this headstone out here, and sometimes, people think I'm a celebrity.

Oh.
The Family
ADDAMS

So, when were you going to tell me that you can read minds?
As soon as I knew I could trust you to not freak out about it.

Anyway, it's not like I can do it with everyone. Or all the time.
How come?

The zombie phenomenon that lets me subconsciously keep tabs on my body also gives me ESP with my fellow dead humanoids, if I concentrate...

... but it ONLY works on the dead, not the living.
No kidding. It works on ANYONE who's dead?

What's Confucius thinking right now?
Big man saw logs. Little man chop sticks.

Nah. Really, what's he thinking?
Rice cakes dishonor both rice and cake.

What ho, Serpent of mischief!
This had better be a zealous gardener practicing speaches for his earth worms or he and I are going to have words.
Oooo

Sayest thou naught in your own defense before I thrash you?
You must be the young man who broke my window.

I don't suppose you're here to give me money for damages and a sincere apology.
Apology? Nay! You hold my lady captive in yon studio apartment and I shall baptize my weapon in your blood.

Well, aren't you precious! You think you're armed and dangerous.

Would you care to trade swords? You might get a fairer fight that way.
Yipe!

SWOON!
RETREAT!

Remember kids, your enemy may not use a sword. Don't assume he can't.

I got a phone call today from animal control saying they'd take my dog away if he keeps scaring people. I assume they meant you.
It's possible.

Never been mistaken for a dog, though. Most city people think I'm a bear or a cow.
I wish you wouldn't take risks by interacting with the mortals like that.

There are way too many of them who'd like to study you, kill you, train you or breed you if they ever found out about you.

Breeding wouldn't be so bad as long as they find me a pretty girl who doesn't smoke.
Cute.

On guard, Beast of Beelzebub!
There you are. I thought I scared you away.

I retreated for a time, but behold, I have retrieved a mighty weapon with which to try your strength.
Very pretty.

Cower in fear, you ugly brute! How dare you make light of my challenge?

Because I know a sharp warrior with a poor sword is better than a poor warrior with a sharp sword.

You've got a nice, sharp sword, Slim, but you've never so much as opened a box with it.
Enough of your riddles and your insults. Answer my challenge at once!
Okay.

I wish you would have shown me that trick on the cheap sword.
Next time, come armed with a pork chop. We can have a dual and a picnic.

Do you know what "Quixotic" means?
Sure do.

It's relating to or having the attributes of the tragic literary figure Don Quixote.

But I've never fought a windmill or bored bitsy school children to tears with my story.
You know what I mean.

You're stubbornly behaving in ways you want to regardless of consequences.

And the world won't let you get away with it.
I am getting away with it.

Well, I am as broke as a 3 year old, Taiwanese condom in the hands of a love-starved teenager with a frozen banana.
But life won't always be the way it is now.

Please?! I'll keep him on a leash. I'll buy him a kennel.
Sorry, Little Lady. An animal like this belongs to the world.
But...

Now hold still, Big Fella. We need your picture for NATIONAL GEOGRAPHIC, TAXIDERMY 'R' US, and anyone else we think should have it.

NO!

LEAP!
FLASH!
THUD!

You know vampires are transparent in photographs, right?
I forgot.

Far be it from me to criticize your "worst case scenario," but don't you think you're being a little overdramatic?
My first draft involved puppets.

Hi. My name is Sarah. It means "lady."
My name is Mary. It means "My mother was raised Catholic."

I'd like to talk to you about how to recieve eternal life.

Does it require a bloodpact with the darkest of dark spirits and the forces of evil at large?

No. The Latter day saints.
Gulp.

Why do you want to redeem me, Sarah? I've never met you.
But you know my fiancé, Steve.

Woah, Steve's getting married?! That was fast. You must be quite a girl.
Thank you.

We met at church. He was sad and angry about the way you treated him. Now that he's saved and we're soulmates, he's happy, and he feels sorry for you.

Did Steve mention the reason we didn't get along is that he wanted to stab me in the heart?

That's silly. God wouldn't let me love a man like that.
Say "We don't want kids," or I'm having your tubes tied around his neck.

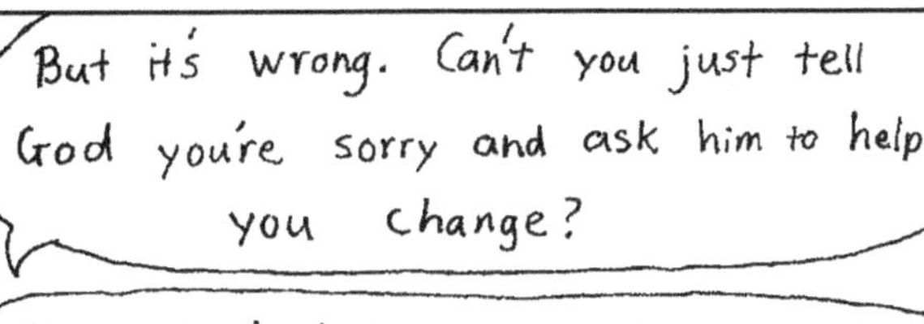

But it's wrong. Can't you just tell God you're sorry and ask him to help you change?

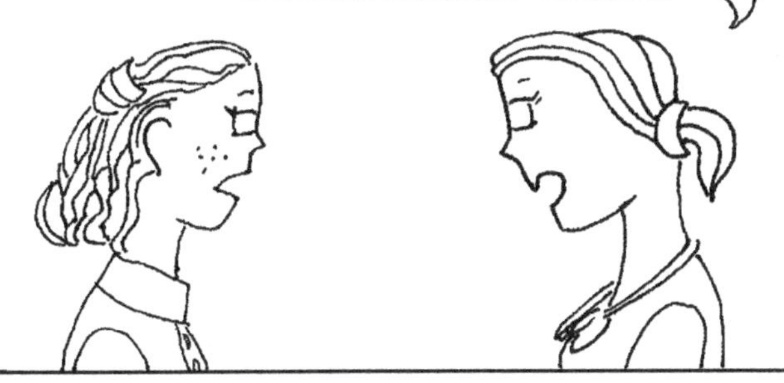

Dear Girl, being a vampire is not just a bad habit like blaspheming or nail biting.

Like vegetarianism, it starts out as a choice. Then, at some point, we can't eat like we did before or we'll get sick.

You can make substitutes like the vegetarians do. They say the veggie versions are better than the meat ones.
Really?

Which part of the lettuce head do you think would make good bacon?
Um, the abs?
Negative.

If you think making loathsome vegetable substitutes for burgers, bacon, and cheese is any less contemptible than my thinning out the human herd from time to time, you're mistaken.

Elder Cooper, is imbibing blood really more grievous to God than veggie bacon?
I wonder if I could get away with a good old-fashioned "Shut up, kid."

Mythfits

I heard Pepper left for good this time.
We can hope but never assume.
What did they finally get her on? Neglegence? Manslaughter?

Maternity.
What?
If HR had anything to do with it, she won't admit it. She's telling everyone she's leaving because she's pregnant.

WHAT?! That snotty, ignorant embodiment of everything wrong with womanhood is allowed to reproduce whenever she wants? There ought to be a law!
Calm down, Mary. It'll be okay. Look, I brought you some happy pills.

Something hallucinogenic, I hope.
No. Just ibuprofen with a smiley face drawn on it.

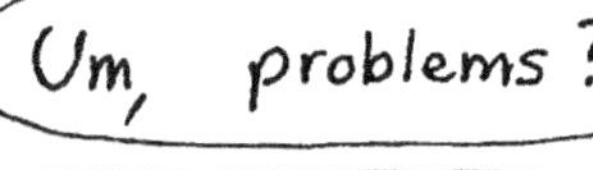

Um, problems?
A stupid, bad-tempered bully of a woman left work this week because she's going to have a baby.

And that bothers you?
It did. Then, I heard my id say, "Cheer up, Mary. Maybe she'll die during childbirth."

DID you cheer up?
Ya-huh. THAT bothered me, too.
What did your superego say?

Nothing. It just shook its head and marveled at how roomy and picnic-like the handbasket to hell is.
Most people don't get in head first.
Which part of me would Satan prefer?

Hey, Doc, Want to sign Pepper's Card?
I Suppose.

It's hard to envision Pepper with a baby. She doesn't seem like the mothering type.
She isn't. She's having the company baby.

ANTIBODIES has a company baby?
We may have several, someday. For now, we're paying Pepper to carry a kid to term.

For what?!
Experiments, I guess. Dr. S. is a paltry #8 on the TOP TEN CRIMES AGAINST HUMANITY list. Maybe he's going for #3 or better.

Why don't you DO something?! Your his partner, aren't you?
I'm a junior partner in a peer's establishment. Until I'm a Senior partner, it's his rules, her body, and none of my business.

And it's not like the kid can complain. He wouldn't even be alive if it wasn't for us.
A week ago, I put sneezing powder in your surgical mask and felt frightfully guilty. Can we try that again with anthrax?

Ready, Igor?
Yes, Master.
NOW!

THUNDER!
ZAP!

It's alive!
It's ALI-HI-HIVE!
And it uses big words.
Grrr...atitude.
Arrr...
mistice.

And that's pretty much the most asinine thing a doctor ever said to me. How about you?
I couldn't narrow them all down to just one thing if I poured them in a funnel.

REST
Knock, knock.
It's taken

One hour later...
KNOCK, KNOCK, KNOCK.
E-hem, It's TAKEN!
Grr...Ahh!

REST
?!.

At this point, I'd say the good doctor "...do believe in spooks." Do you still want me to mess with him?
Humility is the perfect gift for the man who has everything else.

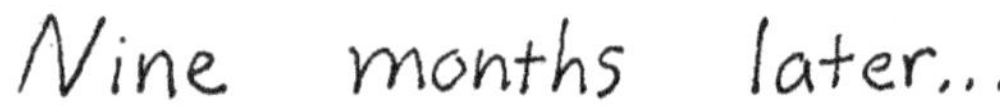

Nine months later...

Hey. Did you hear? Pepper told Dr. S. to go to Hades, and she's keeping the kid.
Bad news for baby but good for her.

She posted pictures online. Wait 'til you see what she had.

It's a gorgon.
And you thought that trip to Crete was just an unbridled waste of company funds.

Want to chip in with me for a mechanical baby swing?
I twelve kinds of don't.
But who more than Pepper deserves a swing and a myth?
Sigh.

Time passes as time only can with a child around, and soon, Pepper needs a babysitter.
STOP!

No, no, no, no! We do not use welding equipment on our toys when there's no adult around.
I was just trying to fix their faces.

What's wrong with them?
None of my dolls look like me. They look like perfect little girls with perfect little complexions and hair, and I can't stand 'em.
Those dolls are pink hunks of plastic that came out of a mold. Just because you're not a pink hunk of molded plastic doesn't mean you're not perfect.

Look, for what it's worth, none of my dolls look like me either. Should we weld on those?
No. We should invent something really neat and get famous. And then, everyone'll want dolls that look like us.
Smooch.

How did a two-faced, curmudgeony wench like Pepper end up with a swell kid like that?
Have we ruled out unprotected sex?

Hey. Can I stay with you 'til Mom gets home?
Sure. School let you out early?

No. I got suspended.
How'd you manage that?

Everyone in class was supposed to turn in a project today. The theme was "Time." So I wrote a story. It was about a vain, vindictive enchantress who could have used her powers to stay young but instead chose to conjure a swarm of tiny, winged beasts to feed on her nemeses' youth and beauty leaving them old and grizzled long before they should be.
She called the beasts "time flies."
So you got suspended for writing Sci-fi?

No. I got robbed. Percy Brown stole my paper and put his name on it. He got an A-.
Why didn't he get suspended?

I knocked him flat and glued a protractor to his belly. You know you can make a sundial out of anything?
Tee, hee, hee! I mean...
Shame on you, Small One.

Big fat liar.
Who's a big fat liar?
MYTHOS

Some lady from the library. She came to my school and started talking about Medea, Medusa, and some of my favorite Greek myths, but she left out important parts of their stories.

Like what?
They LOST! According to her, they met Jason or Perseus or whoever, and they all had a wonderful time I guess, because she refused to talk about all the unhappy endings.

I don't know what to tell you, Kiddo. When we were little, the T.V. told Mary and me about a guy named Faust who sold his soul to the devil and went to Heaven.

I haven't read FAUST, yet. Did he go to Heaven?
Uh, Faust's story is sometimes called THE DAMNATION OF FAUST.

How could grown-ups just flat-out lie to kids like that?
Either to spare our feelings or keep from admitting they'd never actually read the book.

Do you know where gorgons come from?
I... think so. I may have to brush up on some things.

Well, I do, no thanks to Mom. She got all vague and squirmy about the body parts, and I had to look everything up.

It turns out I'm a misfit even by monster standards. Did you know gorgons are supposed to have wings?
Maybe that's a puberty thing.

Okay. So what about my snakes?
Beats me. Weren't you born with them?

I was, but that's not genetic. Gorgons are supposedly born with human-like hair. They get snake nest hair by being rude to Athena, which I wasn't.

My question is what could my mother have possibly done to upset a wisdom godess enough to curse an unborn child?
The lady who until recently thought "penal colony" meant "...like, sex tribe"? Gad only knows.

Um, Petra?

Other little girls who visit ANTIBODIES aren't able to turn our lab rats to stone when they have bad days, and you shouldn't either.
Sorry.

Would you like to talk about it?
I would _like_ to talk to my mom about it, but she won't even look at me.

Well, she _is_ mortal.
Nah, it's more than that. She's great at giving me attention if I'm messing up, but otherwise, she has no time for me.

But she's always taking off work to go to your school stuff. She sees all your pageants, she volunteers for all your field trips...
Exactly. She's a good mother when there's someone around to _watch_ her.

Gad help you if you're a bad parent who raises a kid that's smarter than you.

Suspicious that ANTIBODIES might try to take Petra away, Mary helps Petra learn to protect herself.
Do I have to?

Why can't I start with werewolf deterrents?
Because I can't send a pistol home with a little kid.
Sneak, sneak, sneak.

And why would I have to fight vampires? I don't know any vampires except y'all.
Because the people we don't trust have mind control worms that sometimes get in places they shouldn't. Your attacker could be anyone.
HISS!

EEK!
GASP!
Ahh!

Oh no. No, no, no! I'm so sorry. What do I do now? Do you need 911? CPR?
Petra, calm down. I'm okay.

I'm also relieved and alarmed that your CPR instructor didn't teach you left from right.
Heh·heh. Oops, and you're welcome.

Enraged by the mistreatment of his daughter, Petra's father files suit with ANTIBODIES, pays Pepper off, and takes Petra back to Crete.
If your dad's family treats you like anything less than a princess, you call me, okay?
I will.

Are you going to be okay switching schools mid-year?
I think I may get homeschooled.

Dad says I'm wasting my talents petrifying household pests. Don't know what he thinks my mineral vision is for; turning rat turds into gold for all I know.

Write to me, please. Thank you for being the first grown-up to not disapprove of me.
Thank you for being the first kid I didn't want to throw down a well.

Sentimental much?
No. But I miss Petra.

I do too. But it really is better this way.
I know.

In the states, she'd always be a curiosity at best. In Crete, she'll be a goddess.
With a kid overseas, your friend Pepper might scamper out of the country more often. You think you'll ever miss her?

Odds of my "missing" Pepper are far less than the odds of my hitting her right between the eyes.
As sentimental women go, my sister's about 20% senti- and 80% -mental.
smack!

It's kind of dead in here for a Saturday night, isn't it?
It could be worse.
HOLY Grounds

Last night, some Holy Roller types dropped by to tell me my hat is phallic and ask me how many animals I sacrificed this week.
I'm sorry to hear that.
HOLY Grounds

All of which I could put up with if they'd quit leaving religious pamphlets instead of tips.
I'm sure you could make them uncomfortable enough to leave wanted to. Have you tried threatening to read their coffee grounds?
HOLY Grounds

Close. I told them the shop is made of gingerbread and suggested they should eat it.
HOLY Grounds

No joke. Are love potions real or apocryphal?
They're less apocryphal than Spanish Fly.
HOLY Grounds

You prepare a drink and infuse it with your love for that person, so the potion you make is only as real as your love.
HOLY Ground

If your love isn't real, could bad things happen?
Bad things can always happen, but sometimes, I think a greater power steps in and saves us from our own foolishness.
HOLY

If it didn't, I'd be married to half a boyband, 2 dead actors, and a ninja turtle.
You can't have Raphael. He's mine.
HOLY Ground

We need to start our own religion.
How's that going to help?

Instead of forever getting judged by people with unrealistic standards, we can set the standard and judge 'em right back.

I want to be the high priestess-punisher of bad grammar and punctuation.

What about spelling issues?
Would you sign up for that kind of toil and trouble?

So who's the diety in our fledgeling religion?
Lirdraco.
That sounds ominous and Lovecraftian.

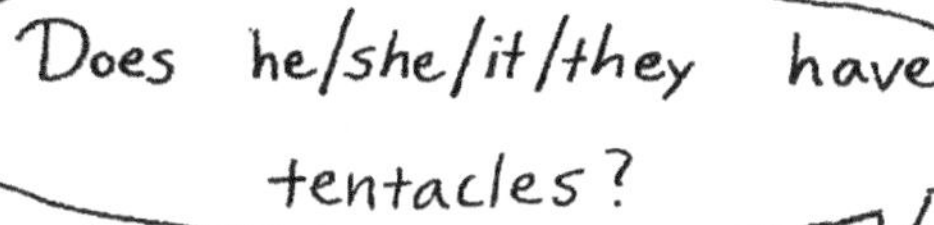

Does he/she/it/they have tentacles?
You could say that. Like most major religions, we'll have elaborate sanctuaries dedicated to a prettier diety with modest shrines to Lirdraco in back of them.

And like those religions our modest shrines will look suspiciously like banks. "Lir-dra-co" is just "Lira, Drachma, and Euro" minced up and jammed together in a made-up name.

So, he/she/it/they has tentacles and green skin?
As befits the god/goddess/totem/pantheon of money and all things "mint" flavored.

This for-profit religion of yours is going to be a tough sell. Lirdracho is an unknown product.
Not for long, but to grow the organization, we'd need to advertise like crazy.
I even came up with the first jingle. Well... "Hymn," I guess.
Dear God I am so scared.

Lirdracho, Lirdracho, best god on the block,
may your flock create havoc on Wall Street today.
Lirdracho, take stock o' all those who would mock.
Other gods forgive debts. You, with cash, make them pay.

A gawker might balk at the shocking Lirdracho.
The faithful bring flow'rs or an over-priced wreath.
Lirdracho's not Spock or the giver of tocos.
Lirdracho's our rock with a jackpot beneath.

Lir...
Stop. No. No more verses, please. There's only so much room in the toilet.
There's room for 3. I measured.

Bits

and Pieces

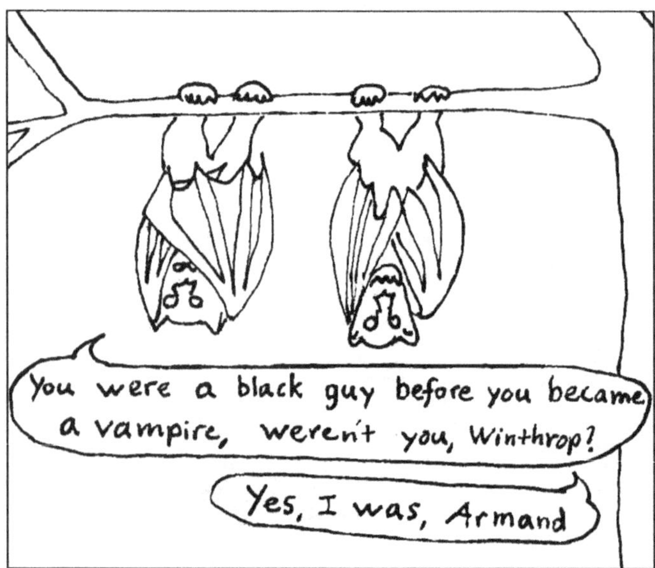

You were a black guy before you became a vampire, weren't you, Winthrop?
Yes, I was, Armand.

In retrospect, is it easier to look back on petty prejudice with a sense of humor?
It's easier in some ways and harder in others.

I think about bats and how if I'm a browner bat than you are, no one thinks twice about our hanging out together.
Bats! Hanging! Ha-HAH!

And if we were still human, I'd hope we could convince the good humans to resist the bad ones and mellow out on the white versus beige versus black attitudes.

Those sound like great ideas, Winthrop.
Thanks, Armand.

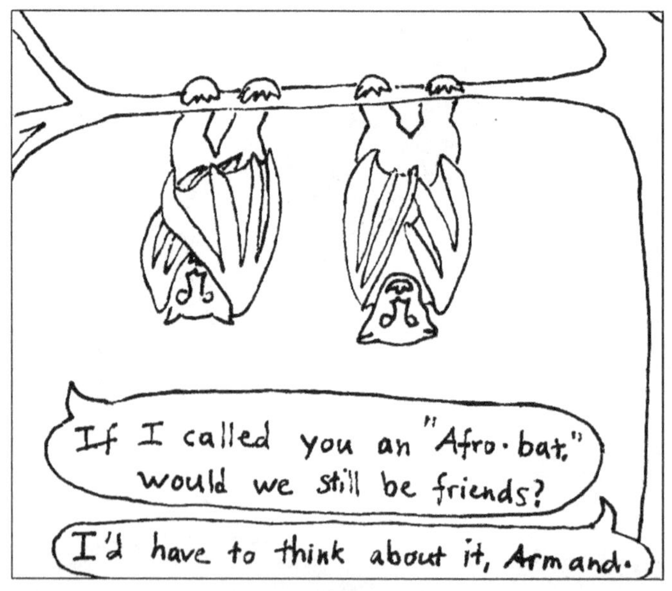

If I called you an "Afro-bat," would we still be friends?
I'd have to think about it, Armand.

Dear Auntie Depressant,
Since turning succubus,
I get sad pretty frequently.
Type, type, type, type.
Type, type.

Holistic healing doesn't help consistantly, and meds don't metabolize right anymore.
Type, type, type, type.
Type, type.
Type, type, type.

If you were me, how would you treat your depression?
Send.
Type, type, type.
Type, type, type.

RE: I'd treat my depression to the same thing that my depression always treats me: Contempt and ice cream.
Ann Landers she ain't.

So, I'm outside the ballpark, and I see this sign that says "Watch out for flying balls and bats."
Yes?

Should I go for the customary innuendos, or should I wait?
Wait.

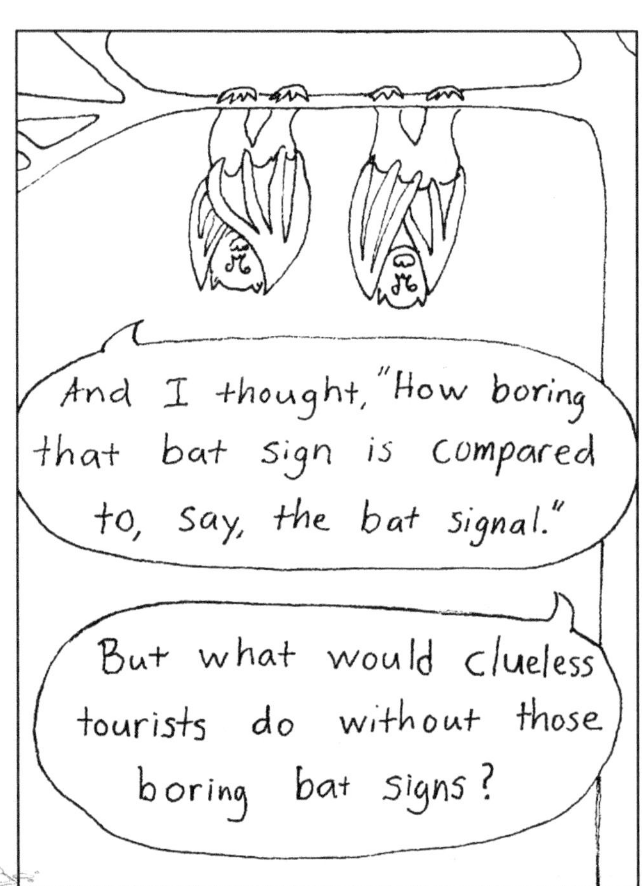

And I thought, "How boring that bat sign is compared to, say, the bat signal."
But what would clueless tourists do without those boring bat signs?

I expect they'd go "POW!" "ZAP," and "SPLAT!"
That's right.

Bat flies into a bar and says, "High balls on me."
Heard it. And it's S'pposed to be a giraffe, not a bat.

2 bat-chelors mosey into a bar. Bartender asks, "Why didn't you fly?" Bat-chelor #1 says "4 balls is a walk."
(Sigh) "Baseball" bats? Really?

Bar flies into a bat...
Now we're talkin'.

"Be a bud. Donate blood."
Catchy, but stupid.

"Be polite when you bite."
Vaguely hooker-ish.

"Show respect. Resurrect?"
No offense, Girly, but I don't think you or FAUST FORWARD are going to come up with the next "Be kind. Rewind."

Do you think we need to explain to some of our not-old readers what "Rewind" means?
I'll bet more than half of 'em could use a refresher on what "Be kind" means.

Ghosts don't need much energy to exist, but they need extra to interact with the world around them.
Chills are the result of ghosts doing something on purpose using human heat energy.

I think we should start a timeshare business with property at the North Pole and South Pole.
Why's that, Armand?

That way, vampires could enjoy 6 sunshine free months at either location and not be driven indoors by light.
Hmm...

I think I saw an outfit like that in a movie already.
Really?

Did they call it "Buy Polar"?
I'd like my mother to be on the posters.

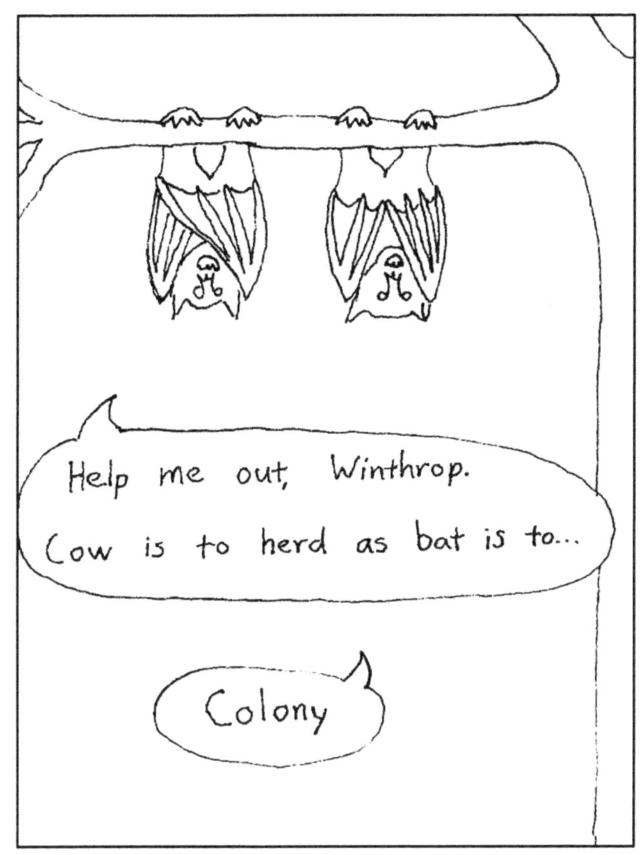

Help me out, Winthrop. Cow is to herd as bat is to...
Colony

That fits. Vampires have colonized the humans for ages.
Have we?

In the sense that we [có·lan·īzd] 'em before we rectum.
Ah.

Potty mouth?
Nein. Fleder mouth.
Sigh. In German.

Dangerous, delightful Delia Druthers,
was a different girl from all the others,
with eyes black as midnight and hair, oh, so red
and tender affection for all things of dread.

While children her age learned of dolls and cat's cradle,
she wove spider webs and tall tales of the fatal,
cruel things her toys had done to toys of her brother's.
"It's not me. It's Barbie," said Delia Druthers.

At sixteen, she, like many girls, became gorgeous.
Unlike them, she poisoned, like one of the Borgias,
each bully and bad boyfriend, hers or another's.
"I thought it was nutmeg," said Delia Druthers.

Dear Auntie Depressant,
In trying to identify patterns in my depressive cycles, I've noticed high days and low days...

And days when I'm knocked flat and looking up at the hairy, incontinent butt of despair.

I'm worried I'll have to deal with feelings like those as long as I exist. Thoughts, please.
Send.

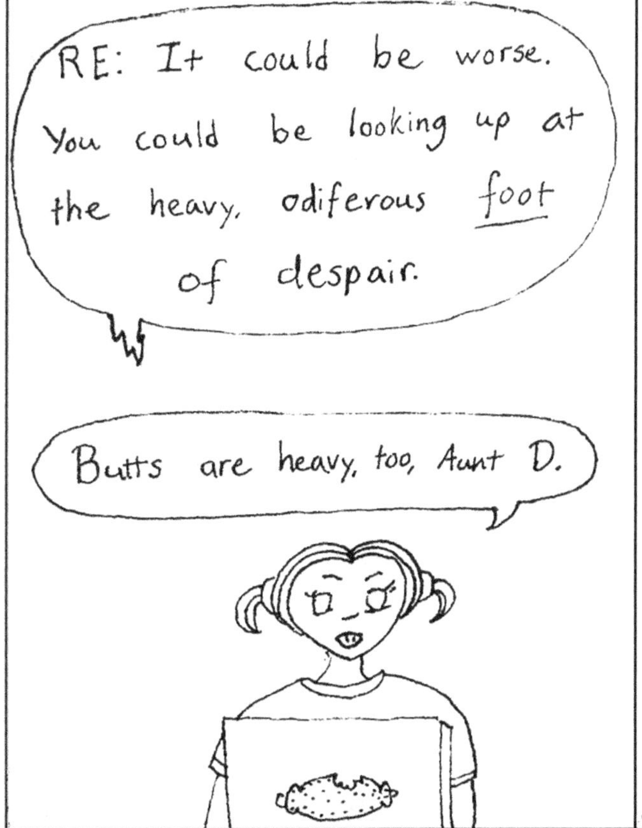
RE: It could be worse. You could be looking up at the heavy, odiferous foot of despair.
Butts are heavy, too, Aunt D.

Am I even allowed to talk to you? I don't want to have to go to another seminar.
I'm okay with it if you are.

I truly don't know how you got accused of harassment when I was the one saying questionable stuff.

Are you mad at me?
Nah. It wasn't that bad

I just sat in the back and drew little cartoon sperms on the seminar brochure.

Dexter, do you like being who you are, or is it just something you've had to get used to?
It's something I've had to get used to...

...But I think we all start out hating who we are a little bit, and we get more comfortable in our own skin over time.

Are there some things that always get on your nerves no matter how well-adjusted you are?
Absolutely.

So help me, if Dr. Love gives me Clap-On lights for Christmas one more time...

On T.V. all the ghosts are preoccupied with crossing over and unfinished business. I never thought I'd meet one so practical joke and breast obsessed.
What can I say? Those things meant a lot to me in life.

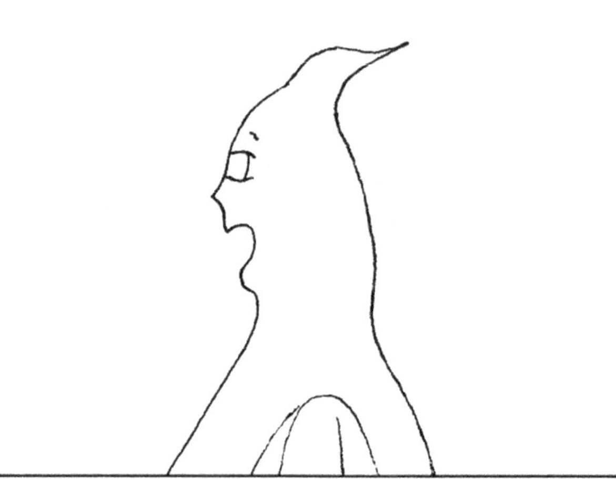

I sometimes think I'd be more mature now if I hadn't died at 17, but I did, and I'm not.

I'm sorry. I forgot who I was talking to for a minute.
It's okay. You didn't hurt my feelings.

Unless you were planning to un-hurt my feelings with a nice, thorough flashing. Then, I'm devastated.
Negative, Ghost Rider.

Is it okay to talk to your family and let them know you're at peace?
Thanks, but no thanks.

My folks don't see me, but I visit them, and they seem less sad.

My sister still yells at me. Anything that goes wrong in our old house, from leaky faucets to bad breath, she blames on me.
Does that hurt your feelings?
Nah. That's just my sister being a sister.

Of course, I being a brother, use my ghostly guile to make the floor boards squeak, then let her wonder how her boyfriend got so farty all of a sudden.

Winthrop, do you ever wish you could be a flying fox?
I'm always foxy in different degrees.

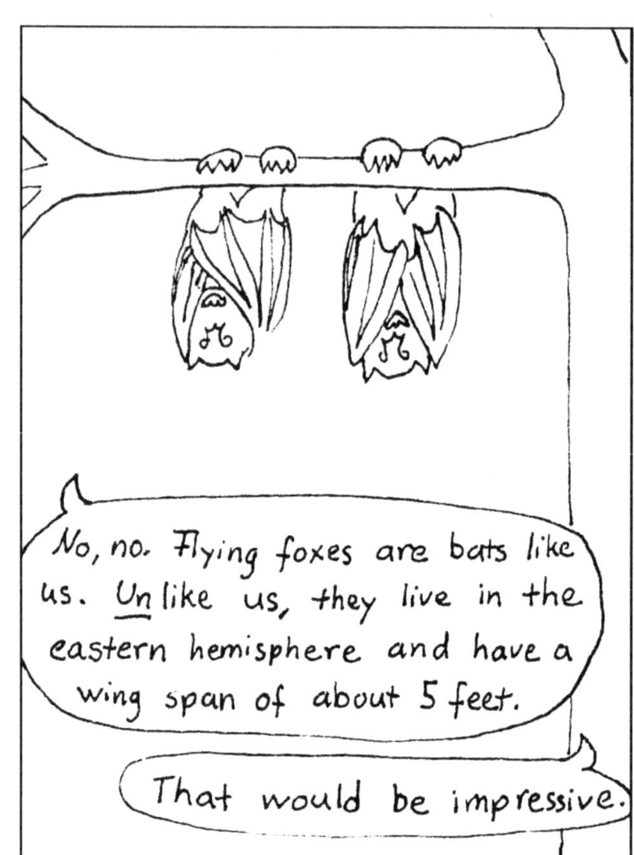

No, no. Flying foxes are bats like us. Unlike us, they live in the eastern hemisphere and have a wing span of about 5 feet.
That would be impressive.

I had a girlfriend who was an expert on flying FAUXs, once.
Sounds like a circus act.

Is it a circus act?
Actually, it's more like an "I'm too tired and bored for this, but I don't want to hurt his feelings" act.

Dear Ms. Meyer,

I've read your work faithfully for the last few years hoping it would get better.

While my hopes have thus-far been dashed, I would like to offer you some commercially sound advice.
Your insipid...
Delete. Delete.
Your books have made trendy the idea of vampires drinking animal blood.
Meanwhile, the processers of hamburgers, steaks, et cetera have buckets of cows blood simply going to waste every day.
If you ask them to sell it as designer, hipster-ish, vampire drinks, you could all make a profit.
You could call it "De-CALF."

I thought you were still bitter about that woman selling more books than you.
Meh. I figure if I could've ridden to fame and fortune on the foppishly sensitive, teen vampire gravy train, I would've.

Heh. "Grave-y train." Get it?
How would you like a kick in the caboose?

A heart loved in bushels and bunches while the body threw nothing but punches.

They fought the same foe, but the heart would lay low 'til the body was knocked on its haunches.

The heart would proceed to defeat every bully it happened to meet.

When the body asked, "How?" the heart took a bow and said, "Hearts break, but hearts also 'beat.'"

It's not exactly THE TELLTALE HEART. Couldn't you give me something a little less sacchrine and a little more horror infused?

Do you want to sell your cheesy merchandise or don't you?
The Beating Heart
The Beating Heart
The Beating Heart
Sigh

Do you find you get less respect from laymen as a chaplain who's physically impaired?
It depends on the laymen

Catholics LOVE me and especially like doing confession with me. They assume I can't hear them since I have no ears.

How DO you hear confession with no ears?

I read lips.
?!

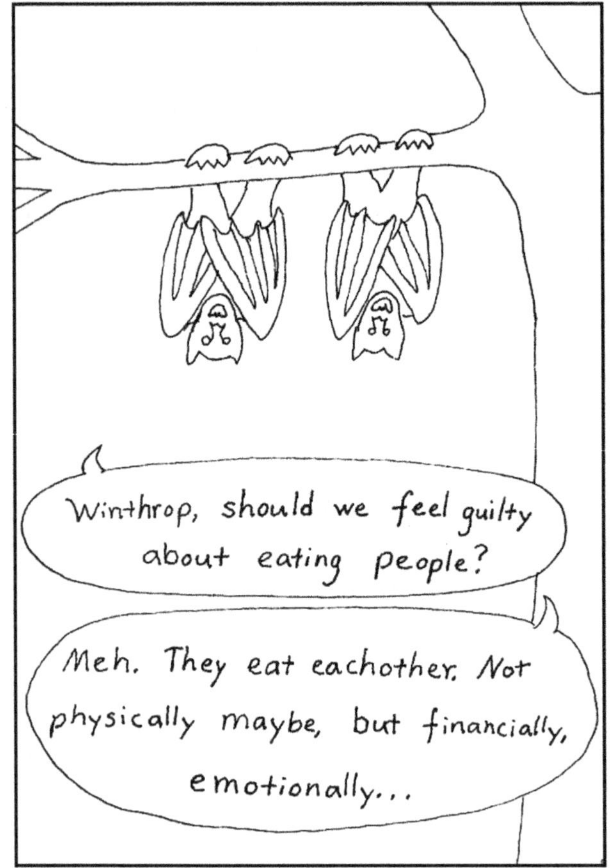

Winthrop, should we feel guilty about eating people?
Meh. They eat eachother. Not physically maybe, but financially, emotionally...

I truly think vampires are to humans what bats are to mosquitoes. Old age won't kill 'em before the population becomes unmanageable, so God lets us do it.

I've eaten mosquitoes before while I've been trying to mingle with other bats.
Oh? What do they taste like?

Mosquite feet, I reckon.
I think I deserve more from you, Armand.

Kat told Matt that Matt's batter fats are that which begat the fatter bats.
That's sad, Armand. Do you know what's sadder?

Stefano from Milano blames Bonno for the guano dawning Don Juan's sauna and piano.
You're right. It is.

You know something, Winthrop? If we had a kids show, we'd have an army of parents ready to kill us.
They'd get over it.

But what, oh what, would happen to the obnoxious plush toy monsters who've been teaching kids to talk in third person all these years?
We'd screw up sometime and find 'em "waiting in the wings." Hah - HAH!

Writer's block, still?
No. It left and came back, so I'm leaving the book alone for now and trying some prose.

There once was a vampire with a heart made of ice who hypnotized mortals into thinking she was nice.
Type. type.
Type. type. type.
Type. type. type.
type. type.

Then, she'd eat them feet first turning grown men to dwarves because toes, feet, and shins were her favorite hors d'oeuvres.
She'd been poisoned and choked. Yet, she always returned. But her wee slaves were cunning, and so they discerned...
Type. type. type.
Type. type.
Type. type. type. type. type.

...if her coffin's oak panels were glass ones instead, by dawn's light, their mistress would surely be dead.
Type. type. type. type.
Type. type. type.
Type. type.
Type. type

"Snow White" is darker when YOU tell it, Big Brother.
I aim to put the "Poe" back in "Poem".
Type. type. type.
Type. type.

I want to write a book for vampires who are new to the whole bat transformation thing.
Why's that, Armand?

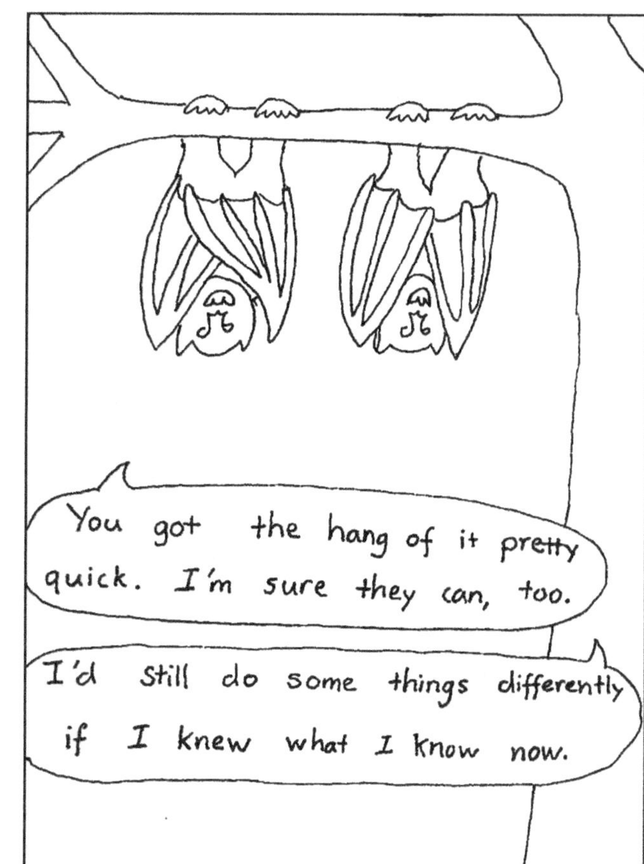

You got the hang of it pretty quick. I'm sure they can, too.
I'd still do some things differently if I knew what I know now.

For one thing, I'd bite at people's legs, then sneak away instead of biting their necks and getting swatted.
Makes sense.

And I wouldn't have to learn the hard way that bats have to turn right side up to pee.
That was just funny.

Say, did you know vampires aren't technically carnivores?
According to What's-her-name, modern vampires are "vegetarians."

No, Seriously. I read it in an article about vampire bats. The ones that eat fruit are called [frook·tə·vorz], and the ones that drink blood are called [săn·gwə·vorz]...

... either of which can fall prey to [dē·vorz].
Which are?

What happen to boy and girl bats with irreconcilable differences.
My brother, the comedian, folks.

Do you get annoyed with tourist-type people who want to talk to you?
Yes and no.
It gets a little old when they ask me to do tricks, but it's nice that they're reaching out and trying to understand.

You've been pretty gentle around me. Would you be capable of poltergeist activity if someone terribly upset you?
That's only happened to me once. Some jerk who doesn't know me said something uncalled-for.

That's a shame. What did he say?
"Elvis' ghost was better."

So, if it's truly better on the other side, why should anyone want to stay here?
Because.
Think about high school. If we gave up back then, we'd have died thinking those were "the best years of our lives," that ketchup was a vegetable, and that THE MATRIX was the greatest movie ever.
I guess so.

Are you sure you're not the ghost of my mother?
Look, I don't know what you're supposed to do here. And unless you know for certain life will not get better, you tend to stay put and assume you have more to do or learn.
...when everyone knows the greatest movie ever was THE MATRIX RELOADED.
Not funny, Mister.
THE WATER BOY?
I don't do exorcisms, but I know people who do!

Do you ever miss being alive?
Not even a little.

Don't get me wrong. I still love the people I loved when I was alive, but basically, having a body is very uncomfortable.

Do you still deal with human emotions, like lust or vengefulness?
Most of those things don't seem that important in hindsight.

...not to say I haven't haunted old girlfriends' underwear drawers now and then.
...haunted the underwear, too.
Yuck.

How are your memorization skills?
I don't consciously memorize much. I just absorb information from my hosts. Why?
If you went into business for yourself, you could make money and eat brains to your heart's content; sell yourself as a learning tool, charm school short-cut, eraser of bad memories... anything that has to do with cerebral function.

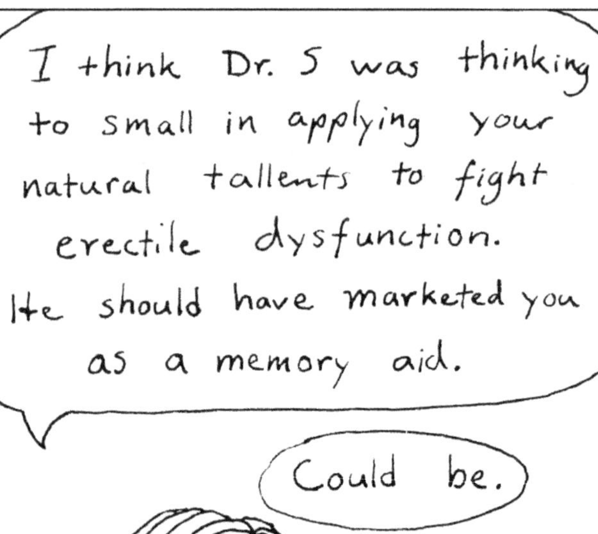

I think Dr. S was thinking to small in applying your natural tallents to fight erectile dysfunction. He should have marketed you as a memory aid.
Could be.
That sounds great, but what would a worm do with money?
Put it on a hook and catch your limit at Lake Stock Exchange?

Look, before you say anything, let me explain a thing or 2, or I'll come to my senses and chicken out.

I've gambled and lost enough with my love life that I know better than to bet on the long-shot.

But that doesn't mean for a single moment I've stopped wanting the long-shot to win.

I know the odds of whatever you and I have working out are hopeless at best, but you're the first girl I've known in a long time who's worth getting hurt for. Waddya say?

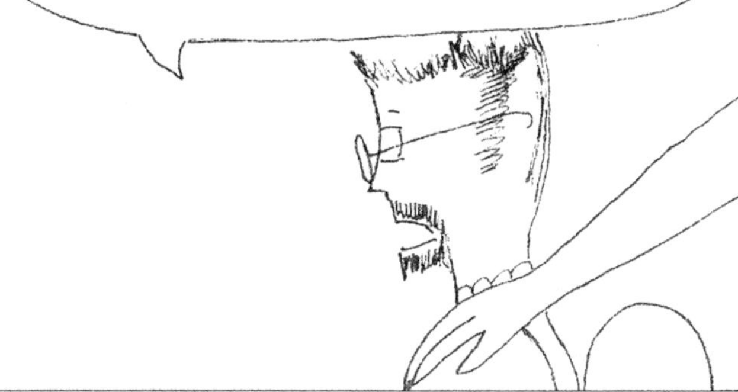

Creek.
Sorry. I was in the bathroom just now. Did you say something?
If you were in the bathroom, who's...
Howdy.

For Gad's sake, Dexter, put some clothes on.
Show some respect, will you? This is my army uniform.

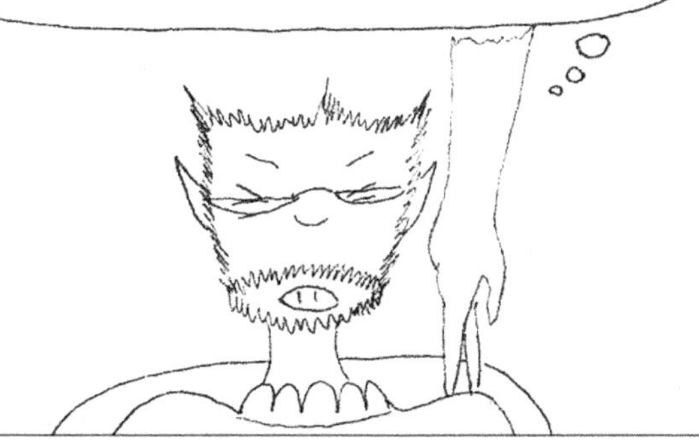

Nice mineral sample. Is it quartz?
I wish.

I saw Dr. Love's new flyer, today. Not only does he have vasectomy coupons marked "Buy one get one FREE," but he's offering a 15% discount every Wednesday, which is, quoth he, "LADIES' NIGHT."

A batch of creep sauce that explains your jagged paperweight how?
Dr. Michaels says I take fools at work too seriously; that I should take everything people like Dr. Love say with a grain of salt.

I'm supposed to take 2 of these and call if my headache doesn't improve.
Might I suggest a taller glass of water?